JALEN'S BIG CITY LIFE

THE PARK CLEANUP

by **Dorothy H. Price** illustrated by **Shiane Salabie**

PICTURE WINDOW BOOKS
a capstone imprint

Published by Picture Window Books, an imprint of Capstone
1710 Roe Crest Drive, North Mankato, Minnesota 56003
capstonepub.com

Library of Congress Cataloging-in-Publication Data
Names: Price, Dorothy H., author. | Salabie, Shiane, illustrator.
Title: The park cleanup / by Dorothy H. Price : illustrated by Shiane Salabie.
Description: North Mankato, Minnesota : Picture Window Books, an imprint of Capstone, 2023. | Audience: Ages 5 to 7. | Audience: Grades K–1. Summary: The local park is a mess, and J.C. needs volunteers to clean up the litter and help the unhoused people living there.
Identifiers: LCCN 2022045539 (print) | LCCN 2022045540 (ebook) ISBN 9781484680926 (hardcover) | ISBN 9781484680865 (paperback) ISBN 9781484680872 (pdf) | ISBN 9781484680896 (kindle edition) ISBN 9781484680919 (epub)
Subjects: LCSH: Urban parks—Juvenile fiction. | Voluntarism—Juvenile fiction. Homeless persons—Juvenile fiction. | Helping behavior—Juvenile fiction. CYAC: Urban parks—Fiction. | Parks--Fiction. | Voluntarism—Fiction. | Homeless persons—Fiction. | Helpfulness—Fiction.
Classification: LCC PZ7.1.P752828 Par 2023 (print) | LCC PZ7.1.P752828 (ebook) DDC 813.6 [E]—dc23/eng/20230109
LC record available at https://lccn.loc.gov/2022045539
LC ebook record available at https://lccn.loc.gov/2022045540

Editorial Credits
Editor: Alison Deering; Designer: Jaime Willems;
Production Specialist: Whitney Schaefer

Design Elements
Shutterstock: Alexzel, Betelejze, cuppuccino, wormig

Printed and bound in the USA. PO#5425

TABLE OF CONTENTS

MEET J.C.

Hi! My name is Jalen Corey Pierce, but everyone calls me J.C. I am seven years old.

I live with Mom, Dad, and my baby sister, Maya. Nana and Pop-Pop live in our apartment building too. So do my two best friends, Amir and Vicky.

MOM

MAYA

DAD

NANA

POP-POP

AMIR

VICKY

My family and I used to live in a small town. Now I live in a city with big buildings and lots of people. Come along with me on all my new adventures!

Chapter 1

THE PARK PROBLEM

J.C. walked to school with
Dad, Amir, and Vicky every day.
They passed apartment buildings
and subway stations. They also
passed the neighborhood park.

The park needed a cleanup. It was full of litter. Flowers were dying. There were also people living in tents.

"Do those people sleep in the park?" Vicky asked.

Dad nodded. "They must be unhoused," he said. "That means they have no home."

"No home!" J.C. exclaimed.

That made him sad. In his old neighborhood, his family had lived in a house. Their apartment in the city was smaller, but it was a home.

"Maybe we can come up with a plan to clean the park *and* help people," J.C. said.

Dad smiled. "That's a wonderful idea. We can ask other people to volunteer too."

"What's a volunteer?" Amir asked.

"Someone who gives their time to help those in need," Dad explained.

J.C. had never volunteered before, but he wanted to help.

"We can all be volunteers!" he exclaimed.

Chapter 2

VOLUNTEERS NEEDED

At school, J.C. and his friends told their teacher about the park.

"We need volunteers to help clean it up," J.C. said.

"I'll help," Mrs. Rowe offered. "Let's start with a list of things you want to get done."

"We know we want to pick up litter and plant flowers," Vicky said.

"We want to help the people without homes too," Amir said.

"I volunteer with a group in my neighborhood," Mrs. Rowe said. "I'm sure they'll help. We can also ask people to donate supplies."

"Like what?" J.C. asked.

"Socks, hats, and gloves," Mrs. Rowe explained. "Those are all things unhoused people need, especially when it's cold."

"That sounds like a great
idea," J.C. agreed.

"Let's do the cleanup next weekend," Mrs. Rowe suggested. "That will give us time to get supplies."

J.C. grinned. "We've got a plan!"

Chapter 3
THINGS TO DO

"We want to clean up the park next weekend," J.C. told his family after school. "Mrs. Rowe will help. She works with a group that helps unhoused people."

"I'd love to plant some fall flowers," Nana offered.

"You know I'll be there," Pop-Pop said.

Amir and Vicky came over later. J.C. and his friends made a list of the things to do. They numbered the tasks. J.C. added names next to each one.

"That looks like a good list," Mom said.

"We need to ask for donations too," Vicky said.

"Things like warm clothes," Amir added.

"Why don't we make a flyer?" Dad suggested. "We can hang it in our lobby. People can sign up."

"Then we'll have lots of
volunteers," J.C. said.

The rest of the week was
busy. Mrs. Rowe talked to her
neighborhood group. They
agreed to help J.C. and his
friends collect donations.

Mom and Dad bought supplies like gloves and trash bags. Nana and Pop-Pop found fall flowers to plant. At the end of the week, the volunteer list was *full*!

TO DO:
☐ 1. Plant Flowers
   Nana and Pop-Pop
☑ 2. Pick Up Litter
   Mom and Dad
☐ 3. Gather Supplies
   Mrs. Rowe
☑ 4. Hang Flyers
   Jalen, Amir, and Vicky
☐ 5. Organize Volunteers
   Nana and Pop-Pop
☐ 6. Distribute Supplies
   Mrs. Rowe
☐ 7. Fill Trash Bags
   Volunteers
☐ 8. Drive Trash to Dump

Chapter 4

CLEANING UP

On Saturday, everyone met

at the neighborhood park.

"I have garbage bags for

litter," Dad said.

"Pop-Pop and I will start planting flowers," said Nana.

"Maya can help us," said Pop-Pop.

Mrs. Rowe came with her volunteer group. They set up a table. J.C., Amir, and Vicky helped with the donations. People could take what they needed.

Everyone worked hard all day.

When they were done, the litter

was gone—and so were all the

donations.

"This was a great idea,"

Amir's mom said.

"I'm proud of you kids for wanting to help," Vicky's dad added.

J.C. and his friends smiled. The park cleanup was a success.

"Thanks to everyone who volunteered!" J.C. exclaimed.

GLOSSARY

donate (DOH-nayt)—to give something as a gift

flyer (FLY-uhr)—a printed piece of paper that tells about an upcoming event

litter (LIT-ur)—pieces of paper or other garbage that are scattered around carelessly

supply (suh-PLY)—an item needed to do a job or task

task (TASK)—a piece of work that has been assigned or needs to be done

volunteer (vol-uhn-TIHR)—a person who offers to do something without pay

unhoused (uhn-HOHZD)—not having a home or place of shelter

BEING A VOLUNTEER

There are many ways to volunteer. What are some things you and your friends could do to help people where you live? Write a list and add tasks next to each name. Share your list with your parents and see if you can make a change like J.C. and his friends!

LET'S TALK

1. Do you ride the bus to school or walk like J.C.? Have you done both? Which do you like best? Why?

2. J.C. feels sad when he sees unhoused people in the park. Have you ever seen unhoused people where you live? How did it make you feel?

3. J.C., his friends, and family decide to help by volunteering. Have you ever volunteered? What did you do? If not, what would you like to do?

LET'S WRITE

1. Do you think J.C., Vicky, and Amir will volunteer again? List some other ways they could help in their neighborhood.

2. J.C. asked for help to make his idea work. Have you ever needed help from others? Try writing a list of of people you could ask for help.

3. J.C and his friends collected items like socks, hats, and gloves. What else do you think they could have collected? Write a list of items.

Dorothy H. Price loves writing stories for young readers. Her first picture book, *Nana's Favorite Things*, is proof of that. A 2019 winner of the We Need Diverse Books Mentorship Program, Dorothy is also an active member of the SCBWI Carolinas. She hopes all young readers know they can grow up to write stories too.

Shiane Salabie is a Jamaica-born illustrator based in the Philadelphia tristate area. When she moved to the United States, she discovered her first true love: the library. Shiane later realized that she wanted to bring stories to life and uses her art to do so.